The Big Island Burglary

Don't miss a single

Nancy Drew Clue Book:

Nancy Drew

* CLUE BOOK *

#14

The Big Island Burglary

BY CAROLYN KEENE * ILLUSTRATED BY PETER FRANCIS

Aladdin

NEW YORK   LONDON   TORONTO   SYDNEY   NEW DELHI

ALADDIN

An imprint of Simon & Schuster Children's Publishing Division
1230 Avenue of the Americas, New York, New York 10020
First Aladdin paperback edition July 2020
Text copyright © 2020 by Simon & Schuster, Inc.
Illustrations copyright © 2020 by Peter Francis
NANCY DREW, NANCY DREW CLUE BOOK, and colophons are registered trademarks of Simon & Schuster, Inc.
Also available in an Aladdin hardcover edition.
All rights reserved, including the right of reproduction in whole or in part in any form.
ALADDIN and related logo are registered trademarks of Simon & Schuster, Inc.
For information about special discounts for bulk purchases, please contact Simon & Schuster Special Sales at 1-866-506-1949 or business@simonandschuster.com.
The Simon & Schuster Speakers Bureau can bring authors to your live event. For more information or to book an event contact the Simon & Schuster Speakers Bureau at 1-866-248-3049 or visit our website at www.simonspeakers.com.
Series designed by Karina Granda
Book designed by Heather Palisi
The illustrations for this book were rendered digitally.
The text of this book was set in Adobe Garamond Pro.
Manufactured in the United States of America 0620 OFF
2 4 6 8 10 9 7 5 3 1
Library of Congress Cataloging-in-Publication Data
Names: Keene, Carolyn, author. | Francis, Peter, 1973- illustrator.
Title: The Big Island burglary / by Carolyn Keene ; illustrated by Peter Francis.
Description: New York : Aladdin, 2020. | Series: Nancy Drew clue book; #14 |
Audience: Ages 6 to 9. | Audience: Grades 2-3. | Summary: Vacationing on the Big Island of Hawaii with friends George and Bess, elementary school student Nancy Drew searches for clues in the case of the missing camera.
Identifiers: LCCN 2019026968 (print) | LCCN 2019026969 (eBook) |
ISBN 9781534442672 (paperback) | ISBN 9781534442689 (hardcover) |
ISBN 9781534442696 (eBook)
Subjects: CYAC: Mystery and detective stories. | Hawaii—Fiction. | Cameras—Fiction.
Classification: LCC PZ7.K23 Be 2020 (print) | LCC PZ7.K23 (eBook) | DDC [Fic]—dc23
LC record available at https://lccn.loc.gov/2019026968
LC eBook record available at https://lccn.loc.gov/2019026969

* CONTENTS *

Chapter

THE MARVELOUS MANTAS

Nancy Drew and Bess Marvin peered over the side of the boat. The water was so dark, they couldn't see anything below the surface. Bess clutched her life vest and stared at Nancy.

"Do you think there are sharks?" she asked nervously.

"Of course there are sharks. It's Hawaii!" George Fayne called out behind them. She leaned back in her seat and shrugged.

"Stop scaring your cousin," Mr. Fayne said.

"We're all going to be just fine. You think I brought you out here to get eaten?"

Nancy looked off into the distance. Up ahead, a few other boats had anchored in a cove and a bunch of people had jumped into the water. They were all wearing life vests and snorkel masks. As soon as she saw them, Nancy wasn't worried. Some of the kids in the groups looked like they were only six or seven. They were smiling and laughing.

They didn't seem nervous about getting into the ocean at night.

"What do the manta rays look like?" George asked their boat's captain. "Are they gray like sting rays?"

Captain Tane shook his head. "They're black and white. They have spots on their bellies and huge mouths. That's how they eat the plankton."

"What's plankton?" Nancy asked. She'd heard that word before, but realized she didn't really know what it meant.

"Plankton is what a lot of the big fish feed on," Captain Tane said, scratching his goatee as he steered the boat. He was a round man with thick black hair. "It's lots of tiny sea creatures—eggs and little crustaceans. They're so small, you can't see them."

"Can the manta rays' tails hurt us? Are they sharp?" Bess asked. She was still staring into the water, looking worried.

"Nah. They don't have barbs or stingers. The mantas are gentle creatures," Captain Tane said. "They're called the 'butterflies of the ocean.' I think you're going to love them."

That seemed to make Bess feel better. Ku, the first mate, passed her a pair of flippers, and she sat down on the bench to put them on. Soon their boat was gliding into the cove to join the others.

Nancy had only been snorkeling once before, with her dad. When George's parents invited her on their summer vacation to Hawaii, she knew it would be the first for a lot of things. From the moment they stepped off the plane, it had been nonstop fun. They were staying on the Big Island, which was just like its name—the biggest island in the Hawaiian island chain—and there was so much to do and see. On Sunday, they'd taken surfing lessons. Nancy had even managed to get up on the board and surf a tiny wave all the way to shore. Then Mrs. Fayne took them on a long hike through the jungle. It was so green and beautiful, Nancy felt like she was walking through a movie set. Tomorrow, they were going to a luau, which was a special Hawaiian feast.

That night, Mrs. Fayne and Scotty, George's three-year-old brother, stayed back at the hotel.

Scotty was way too young to swim with manta rays, and Mrs. Fayne seemed happy to have an excuse not to go. Nancy wondered if she was as nervous as they were about getting into the water at night.

"What are those for?" Mr. Fayne asked.

As they got closer, they could see that each group had a guide and a surfboard covered in blue lights. The water in the cove was glowing.

"Blue lights attract plankton," Ku said. "The manta rays will swim up for a snack. You just have to hold on to the board. Then you watch and wait."

"Everyone ready?" Captain Tane asked. He parked the boat beside the others.

George was still fiddling with her snorkel, and her dad had to adjust the strap for her. "Ruddy as ull avaa beee," she said through the mask.

Ku climbed down the ladder at the back of the boat and plunged into the water. He was short and muscular, and was such a good swimmer, he didn't need a life vest. He pulled the surfboard down with him and turned on the blue lights.

"This is going to be great, girls," Mr. Fayne said as he jumped in behind Ku. He grabbed on to the surfboard, which had handles along the sides. They waved for Nancy and her friends to follow.

"Eeeeeeeeeek!" Bess let out a squeal as she jumped in.

Nancy and George climbed down the ladder and swam out to the surfboard. The water wasn't as cold as Nancy thought it would be. All around them, people floated onto their bellies, their masks in the water as they waited for the manta rays.

"Hold on with both hands, just like this," Ku said as he grabbed two handles on the side of the board. He kicked his legs and lay flat.

Nancy and Bess went on one side of the surfboard and George and her dad went on the other. They stared into the water below. Nancy could hear each of her breaths through the snorkel.

They waited . . . and waited. Nancy started to

get a little cold and suddenly wished she'd worn the wet suit Ku had offered her.

All around them, other groups clustered around their surfboards. Just when Nancy was sure nothing was going to happen, she saw something swimming toward them.

"Ahhhhhhhrrrghh!" Bess yelled through her snorkel.

As the creature got closer, Nancy saw its huge, gaping mouth. It was like a giant sting ray. Its mouth was so big, it looked like it could swallow Nancy whole.

Nancy raised her head from the water, suddenly nervous. George and her dad were both still floating on their stomachs and watching the manta. She put her head back down so she wouldn't miss anything.

The creature swam closer and closer, and Nancy's stomach twisted into knots. It was so huge and coming right toward her. When it was a few feet away, it dipped down under them and did a backflip. Its belly was covered with dozens of black spots!

Nancy could see into its gills as it flipped around again and again, taking in huge mouthfuls of plankton. A second manta ray swam up next to it and started doing the same thing. She understood now why people called them "the butterflies of the ocean." They were so graceful. With all their flipping, it seemed like the manta rays were dancing together.

The group kept watching for almost an hour. When the first manta rays swam off, new ones swam over, feeding on the plankton beneath the board. Every minute was better than the last. Ku and Captain Tane had to call Nancy and Bess several times before they picked their masks up out of the water.

"That was incredible!" Bess said.

"Amazing," Nancy agreed.

As they swam back to the boat, Nancy couldn't stop smiling.

Chapter

HULA THE NIGHT AWAY

"Aloha," a woman in a colorful straw skirt said. She hung a flower garland around Nancy's neck. "Come in. Welcome!"

"Mahalo," Nancy replied. Just that morning, she'd learned the Hawaiian word for "thank you." She'd used it after she bought a coconut on the beach, and when Bess helped her take her snorkel off.

George looked around the patio, which was lit by tiki torches. "It's magical. . . ." A few of the women who worked at Sunrise Resort were now wearing hula skirts and huge, leafy green leis around their necks. Onstage, three men were playing giant drums as another man spun fire on a string. When the fireball moved through the air, it created different shapes—circles and figure eights. It was one of the coolest things Nancy had ever seen.

"Do you believe this dinner?" Mrs. Fayne asked, handing plates to each of the girls. "I don't think I've ever seen a roast pig before."

They walked down along the long buffet table. A whole pig had been roasted on a spit and was

now sitting there with an apple in its mouth. A woman with a short black bob carved steaks off a giant white fish, and there were piles and piles of brightly colored fruits. There was probably enough pineapple to last a year.

"Whoa! What's that?" Nancy asked, staring at what looked like a bowl of purple mashed potatoes.

"This is poi," a skinny, shaggy-haired man behind the table explained. His name tag said TED. "It's made out of taro root. Want to try some?"

Nancy and Bess both held their plates up, and Ted scooped some onto each. The girls liked the idea of eating something new, especially a pretty purple food. When would they get the chance to do that again?

Nancy loaded her plate with poke, a traditional Hawaiian dish made up of raw fish, soy sauce, salt, and onions. She even took a few slices of roast pig, but she had to look away when they served it. She kept thinking the pig was staring at her.

When they found their table, it was right in

the front row. Mr. Fayne and Scotty had come down to the luau a little early to find a spot. Mrs. Fayne frowned when she noticed Scotty's plate. It just had one big pile of strawberries.

"He refused to eat anything else!" Mr. Fayne laughed.

George rolled her eyes. "Scotty's going to turn into a giant strawberry. . . ."

"Am not," Scotty whined, then popped another berry into his mouth.

"You're definitely going to get seconds, mister," Mrs. Fayne said, sitting down beside him. "But look at this view. Lucky us."

"I can feel the heat!" George said, holding up her hands. The dancer swung the fireball around and around just a few yards away.

A bald man in a flowered shirt sat at the next table snapping dozens of pictures. He aimed his giant camera at his two teenage kids, then at his redheaded wife, then at the man spinning fire. It seemed like he was trying to capture every single second of the show.

"Dad, stop it," the teenage girl said, holding up her hand to block the camera. She had long brown hair and freckles, and wore purple high-top sneakers. Her brother was a foot taller than her. His black fauxhawk was gelled into place.

"And now, for what's sure to be your favorite part of the evening," the emcee announced, "the hula show! Can we have a few volunteers come up here to help us out?"

Bess's hand shot up. She was more excited than she'd been all day.

"Yes, the young lady in the front!" The emcee was wearing a teal suit and tie. He pointed to Bess. "Would your friends like to join you?"

Nancy and George shook their heads. The luau was packed—there must've been two hundred people there. Nancy was getting stage fright just thinking about standing up in front of everyone.

"Come on. Please?" Bess begged. She grabbed Nancy's arm. "I can't go up there alone."

Nancy could feel the entire crowd looking at

them. They'd spent the afternoon snorkeling at the beach, but that hadn't really been Bess's thing. Her mask kept getting fogged up and she'd been worried that a giant sea turtle they'd seen was going to bite her. Maybe doing the hula with Bess wouldn't be so bad. . . .

George shook her head again. "No way, no how! I'm not doing the hula in front of everyone." She laughed, and her brown eyes went wide.

"Okay, I'll go with you," Nancy agreed. Bess nearly shrieked with delight as the girls made their way onto the stage. Bess was wearing her new dress, which had tiny palm trees all over it, and she fixed the skirt so it fell perfectly in place.

The emcee also pulled up the bald guy from the table next to them and an elderly couple from way in the back. He asked a set of triplets two tables over to come up, but they were too shy. The littlest one clung to his seat when the emcee came near him.

When Nancy looked out into the crowd, her hands started sweating. Everyone was watching them. She tried to focus on the two hula dancers who were showing them the moves, but she was only half paying attention. She'd never been onstage in front of so many people.

"Are you ready?" the emcee asked.

Nancy wasn't so sure, but then the music started, and everyone swayed their hips back and forth. The two dancers stood a little bit in front of them. One was wearing a blue straw skirt, while the other's skirt was purple, but they both had on colorful flowered tops. They moved their arms gracefully as they took a few steps sideways across the stage.

Nancy and Bess followed their lead. Every time the dancers stretched their arms out to the side, Nancy and Bess stretched their arms out to the side. Every time the dancers spun around, Nancy and Bess spun around. Bess was a natural, smiling and laughing as she did each new move, and soon Nancy was having fun too. By the time the dance was over, she'd forgotten she was even onstage.

"You girls were terrific!" Mr. Fayne said, brush-

ing his floppy brown hair away from his face as
they returned to their seats.

"Wasn't that so fun?" Bess asked, while the
crowd clapped. The girls watched the rest of the
show from their table. Soon, four more dancers went onstage, and they all spun around in a
graceful, choreographed hula dance.

After the show finished, the girls picked

out some desserts from the buffet. Nancy chose kulolo, which was a solid pudding that tasted like coconut. Bess and George both tried the haupia cake, which looked kind of like a birthday cake. Mr. Fayne was the only one who had the malasada, special Hawaiian doughnuts.

"You missed the shaved ice!" Mrs. Fayne called out as she and Scotty caught up with them. Scotty looked mad. His second plate was piled with real food—vegetables, pork, and rice. Mrs. Fayne held up a giant cup covered in fruit and berries. George dug her fork into the bowl and stole a bite.

"Now I didn't miss it," she said, and smiled.

Mrs. Fayne snuck her own spoonful of George's haupia cake. "Yum! This is great inspiration for my catering business. I haven't tried such inventive flavors in a long time."

"The frosting on the cake is the best," Bess said. "It tastes like . . ."

She trailed off as she noticed the bald man yelling about his camera a few yards away. As they got closer, Bess, George, and Nancy could see that his wife and kids all seemed upset too.

"I don't understand," his wife said. "It was here on the chair just a minute ago when you went up to do the hula! I just saw it. Z, double check that it didn't fall under the tables. Maybe someone kicked it aside?"

The teen peered under their table, then under the table where Nancy was sitting. "It's not here, either," he said.

"You're sure you didn't move it, Carol?" the man asked his wife. She shook her head. Then he looked to his daughter. "Can you ask the people at the next table, Lizzy?"

Lizzy glanced around the patio. "Everyone's leaving. . . ."

It was true. Now that the show was over, most people were headed to their rooms.

That only seemed to upset the man more. He paced back and forth, checking under the front of the stage, behind some plants, and beneath Mrs. Fayne's chair. He kept rubbing his temples, like he had a horrible headache.

"My camera!" he finally said. "Someone stole it. . . . It's gone!"

Chapter

3

CAMERA CHAOS

"Are you sure you didn't misplace it?" Mr. Fayne asked, stepping forward to try to calm the man down. "Could it be in your bag?"

The family with the triplets hurried past, staring at the small crowd that had formed around the table.

"It's not. We checked. Harry is very careful with his camera," Carol said. "He's never lost it, not once! Oh, this is terrible. And the pictures from Mom and Dad's party . . ."

Harry put his face in his hands. "I forgot about that! I didn't even get to download them. Now, they're gone forever."

Lizzy turned to them and tried to explain. "My grandparents had a fiftieth anniversary party last week. Dad took all the pictures. He's kind of like our family photographer."

"I didn't save them yet." Harry shook his head. "I was going to do it when we got back home."

"Maybe it'll turn up, Dad," Z tried. "Maybe someone just thought it was theirs."

"Then where are they? Why haven't they come back?" Harry glanced around. Most of the diners had now disappeared. A few lingered by the sofas at the edge of the patio, and a group of little kids were talking to the hula dancers, asking them dozens of questions. Just then, a short, curly-haired woman in a purple Sunrise Resort shirt strolled past, waving to a few of the performers as she went. Nancy had seen her behind the front desk and talking to guests by the pool.

"Miss! Are you the manager?" Carol called out.

The woman paused, turning toward the group. She had a round, heart-shaped face and pretty brown eyes. "I am. What can I help you with?"

Harry gestured to the empty patio. The servers had started pulling apart the buffet and were wheeling off carts of leftover food. "I need you to find all the people who were at the luau tonight. Someone in the crowd stole my camera. Can you call everyone back? Or search their rooms?"

"I'm afraid I can't," the manager said. Nancy noticed her name tag said LULU. "But if you give me your room number, I'll be sure to let you know if anyone brings it to the front desk. Sometimes items turn up in the lost-and-found."

"But what if it doesn't?" Carol asked.

Lulu took out a pad of paper and pen from her back pocket. "We just have to hope for the best. May I have your room number?"

"Two-oh-eight," Harry said. "Can you ask around and see if people saw the camera?"

"I can't question our guests, sir," Lulu said. "Everyone is here to relax and have fun. I'll let my team know to keep an eye out for it, though. Sound good?"

Harry still looked like he might burst into tears, but he managed a small nod.

Lulu walked back toward the front lobby.

"We saved for a whole year to take the kids on this vacation," Harry said, turning to Mr. and Mrs. Fayne. Scotty was so tired, he'd sat down at their feet and was playing with a lei he'd found. "We squirreled away every penny. That camera was pricey, I'm not going to lie. Now I'm going to have to save for the whole next year to replace it."

Harry sat down on one of the last few chairs on the patio, while workers wheeled away two huge round tables. He rested his face in his hands.

"Well, we can help you search if you want," Mr. Fayne said. He glanced sideways at Nancy, Bess, and George.

Nancy smiled. Of course, they could do better

than just help Harry and his family search. At River Heights Elementary, the three girls were known for solving mysteries. Friends and teachers had even started calling them the Clue Crew. Weeks ago, they'd found an expensive telescope when it went missing from the planetarium.

"We might be able to find it," Nancy said, straightening up. "We're always helping friends and teachers with different mysteries, and this is definitely a big one. . . ."

"But you're on vacation," Lizzy said, scraping the toe of her sneaker across the ground. "You really want to look for a missing camera?"

"Yeah, it'll be fun," George said. Nancy could tell she was already surveying the scene for clues. "We only have one day left, though, so we have to get to work as soon as possible."

Carol and Harry shrugged. They waited for Mr. and Mrs. Fayne to say no, or to explain, but the Faynes were used to the Clue Crew jumping in to help. George had once told Bess and Nancy how proud her parents were of them.

"Well, all right," Carol finally said. "I guess it can't hurt."

"No, it can't," Nancy replied. She pulled a notebook out of her back pocket. Across the front, it read *Clue Book*. "Now, let's get to work. . . ."

Chapter

4

TAKING NOTES

Nancy and George sat on the lounge chairs by the pool. They looked at the list in front of them. Nancy had written *MOTIVE* in big block letters at the top of the page. That was just another word for "a reason someone would do something."

"Maybe Lizzy is right," Nancy said, studying the first reason she'd written down. It said *ACCIDENT* in big letters, right under *MOTIVE*. "Maybe this is all a mistake. Someone might have taken the camera by accident."

"Maybe they thought it was theirs," Bess said as she dangled her feet in the pool. Every now and then, she looked across at Mr. Fayne, who was chatting with a few Sunrise Resort employees as they cleaned up the patio. Mrs. Fayne had gone back to the room with Scotty to put him to bed, though she promised to help in the hunt the next day. Nancy, Bess, and George had asked everyone they could find about the missing camera, including a couple on their honeymoon who were in the hot tub and a few loud teenagers in the deep end of the pool, playing a game of Marco Polo.

"If it was really an accident, then we should

know soon," George said. "The person will realize they have the wrong camera. Then they'll return it to the front desk, like the manager said."

"I think we can cross that motive off the list if we don't hear by tomorrow morning," Nancy said. "What else? Why would a camera go missing?"

"It *could* have been stolen. . . ." Bess kicked her feet underwater. "Harry said it's really expensive. Maybe someone took it, thinking they could sell it for a lot of money."

"But who comes all the way to Hawaii to steal a camera?" George asked.

"That's true," Nancy said. "Almost all the people on the patio were other families on vacation. It would be kind of odd, but that doesn't mean someone wouldn't do it."

Nancy wrote down *STOLEN (TO KEEP OR SELL IT)* as another motive. Then she wrote down the last possible motive, *LOST.* She knew that was unlikely.

When Nancy and her friends sat down to take notes, Harry and Carol Hendricks had gone back to the patio to search for the camera again. They wanted to see the Sunrise Resort team take apart the stage in case the camera had fallen and been kicked underneath. Lizzy and Z had left, saying they had to go to a party on the beach down by the surf shack. They'd promised to continue the search in the morning.

George pointed to the other end of the pool. "Here they come." The Hendrickses were walking toward them. Their hands were empty. Mr. Fayne wasn't far behind.

"Nothing!" Harry said as he got closer. He shook his head.

"No one saw the camera." Mr. Fayne shrugged. "And they checked and rechecked all the tables and chairs to make sure nothing got wheeled away that shouldn't have. I'm not sure what else to do."

Nancy crossed the word *LOST* off her list. It was still possible someone had taken the camera by accident, but she knew now it hadn't been misplaced. She flipped to a fresh page.

"Did you notice anything strange tonight? Is

there anyone you remember acting weird?" Nancy asked. Sometimes, when people really thought about it, they remembered new details.

"Hmm . . . ," Carol murmured. "I don't think so."

"Was there anyone you spoke to recently who stood out?" Bess asked.

"Well, now that you mention it," Harry said, "yesterday, some guy at the beach thought I stole his lounge chair. He was older, white hair. Do you think that could be something?"

"But we didn't see him at the luau," Carol said.

"I guess you're right," Harry agreed. "He wasn't there."

"Besides, I don't think he'd take your camera as revenge," George added.

Nancy stared at her blank paper, worried that they still had no real suspects. The lounge chair man couldn't have stolen the camera if he wasn't at the luau. Where would they begin their investigation? The Clue Crew didn't have a single clue.

"It's getting late," Mr. Fayne said. "You girls

should have been in bed an hour ago. I think it's time to put this case on hold until the morning."

Harry nodded, but Carol was staring off into space. Then, suddenly, her blue eyes went bright. "Actually . . . I think I did see something strange!"

"Really? What?" Mr. Fayne asked.

"This woman, she was a little older than me," Carol started. "She was at the luau alone. I remember noticing her because she kept looking over at Harry. Then, at one point, I realized she was watching him take pictures. . . . She was watching his camera."

"What did she look like?" George asked. "Do you remember what was she wearing? Her hair color? Eye color?"

Carol furrowed her brow. "Oh, I don't know. I only saw her for a few seconds. Maybe big sunglasses? I really can't recall."

"She was staring at my camera?" Harry said.

"I think she was!"

"Is there anything else you remember?" George asked. "Are you sure she was alone?"

"I'm definitely sure of that." Carol nodded.

"Okay, girls . . . I'm serious. Bed. Now." Mr. Fayne put his arms around Nancy and George's shoulders and gave Bess a pointed look. "You can start up again in the morning." He turned to the Hendrickses. "It was great to meet you both. We'll see you tomorrow. Don't worry. I'm sure we'll get to the bottom of this."

"Let's hope," Harry muttered.

As they walked off, Nancy was still puzzled. Carol had said the woman she'd seen was older, alone, and maybe wearing sunglasses. Almost everyone at Sunrise Resort had sunglasses, even George (and she hated sunglasses). And half the people at the resort were over fifty.

"At least we have a suspect," George said. "You heard Carol. The woman was staring at Harry's camera!"

"But how are we going to find her?" Nancy asked.

"Don't worry," Bess said. "I have a plan."

Chapter

5

CAUGHT ON CAMERA

The next morning, Nancy and her friends walked down the stone pathway to one of the resort's restaurants. They'd decided to get an early start on the day. While most kids were already in the pool, tossing around a beach ball, Bess was talking her friends through her plan.

"The thing is, everyone at the luau was taking pictures, but most people took them on their phones, not on a giant expensive camera like Harry's."

"His camera lens was five feet long!" Nancy laughed. She was just kidding, but it *was* really big. "He kept switching out different lenses too, like he was a real photographer."

"You're right—lots of people were taking pictures," George added. "Some people even took videos."

"So, we just ask people if we can see their photos from the luau . . . ?" Nancy asked.

"Exactly," Bess replied. "Then we see if we can pick out this strange woman Mrs. Hendricks was talking about. She must be in at least one or two of those photos. Probably more."

"The new cell phone cameras are so good, we can probably zoom in and crop the photo to get a perfect picture of her," George added. She loved technology, and it came in handy when they were investigating.

The girls strolled into Sunrise Resort's biggest restaurant, the Green Pineapple. It smelled like pancakes and eggs. They'd come here every morning since the first day of the trip, piling their plates high with waffles, scrambled eggs, and dragon fruit. Nancy wanted to run over to the buffet and grab a juicy strip of bacon, but she knew she had to stay focused.

"Let's split up," Bess suggested. She waved toward the tables in front of them. "I'll take all the round tables on the right, and, George, you should take all the round tables on the left. Nancy, you can talk to everyone in the booths."

The girls went their separate ways. Nancy approached a family first. The two men had a baby and a toddler with them.

"Can I ask you a question?" Nancy said.

"Sure thing," one of the men said. He had curly hair and was feeding the baby orange mush. "What's up?"

"My friends and I are looking for a woman who was at the luau last night. The only problem is, we don't know her name or what she looks like. But we think someone got a photo of her."

The other man shrugged. He was wearing a bright green shirt and had five o'clock shadow.

"Ahhh . . . we weren't at the luau last night. We had to put these two to bed. We did see the sunset from our balcony, though. . . ." He pulled his phone out of his pocket and showed Nancy a picture of a pink and orange sky. She smiled. It really was a beautiful photo.

"No problem. Thanks," she said as she left them to finish their breakfast.

She tried the next table, but the young couple there said they hadn't taken any pictures at the luau. The next family had a bunch of pictures on the mom's phone, but they were all of her five-year-old eating poi for the first time. It wasn't until Nancy asked a fourth table that she found some useful photos.

"I've gotten pretty good at using this thing," the white-haired woman said. She was seated with an elderly woman with huge pink earrings. "Technology is so wild!"

The woman flipped through dozens of photos, but there were none of the suspect Carol had described. Nancy was just about to try another booth when George called out from a table a few feet away. "Nancy, Bess! I found something!"

Nancy ran to George's side. She was standing with a young African American couple. The man was wearing a Hawaiian shirt, and the woman had on a colorful sundress. Nancy leaned over and looked at the phone screen as the man scrolled through his album.

"That's her! Right there," George said, pointing to a woman in the background. The man handed George his phone and she zoomed in, then cropped the photo and saved a new version of it. Now they could see the mystery woman clearly. She was wearing sunglasses and a straw hat. Wisps of curly blond hair peeked out from underneath the brim.

"I thought she seemed a little odd . . . ," said the man, who'd introduced himself as Paul.

"Do you have any more pictures of her?" Bess asked.

Paul scrolled through his phone and found two more. In the second, the strange woman was scowling at Harry's camera.

"Why do you think she's so angry at Harry?" George asked. "She's definitely looking at the camera in this one. But why? What would she want with it?"

Just then, a waitress came by and picked up the couple's plates. She stared at the phone just a little too long, trying to see what Nancy and her friends were doing. "That's Olivia Andover. She's been coming here for years. Always stays in one of our penthouse suites."

"Really?" Bess asked. "Do you know where she is now?"

"I think I saw her in the spa before," the waitress said. "Why?"

But the girls were too excited to answer. They thanked Paul and his wife for their help as they headed for the door.

The spa was all the way on the other side of the resort, so the girls ran down the stone path, passing two different pools and another restaurant along the way. They stopped right by the gym, where they could see the spa's front desk. Olivia Andover was standing right there. She handed the receptionist her credit card.

"That's her. She must be leaving," Bess whispered. The friends hid in a corridor next to the gym so Ms. Andover wouldn't notice them. She looked exactly like she had in the photos. She was wearing sunglasses and her giant straw hat, even though they were indoors.

She turned to leave, and the girls knew this was their chance. If they didn't confront her now, she might get away. They ran out from around the corner.

"Ms. Andover!" Nancy called out, and the woman turned around. "Can we talk to you for a minute?"

But instead of replying, Olivia Andover darted to the elevator down the hall. She pressed the button again and again until the doors opened. Before Nancy could even get a word out, Ms. Andover had slipped inside.

"I think she just ran away from us!" George said.

"She definitely did." Bess pointed to a door that said STAIRS. "But we know where she's going. I bet we can beat her to the penthouse!"

Chapter

6

RICH AND FAMOUS

Nancy was running so fast, her legs hurt. She wasn't sure how many flights of stairs they'd climbed, but she could barely breathe. Bess reached the top floor first. She grabbed Nancy's hand and helped her up the last steps.

"Come on! I hear the elevator!" Bess cried.

George followed right behind them. Sure enough, every time the elevator passed a floor, it let out a loud *bing!* Suddenly, it was right there, the light above it glowing white. The doors slid back to reveal Olivia Andover. She seemed shocked to see them waiting.

"Please," George tried. "We just want to talk to you."

Olivia stepped back into the elevator and pushed the close button a bunch of times. The doors started to slide shut, but Nancy stuck out her hand to stop them.

"Look, I don't have any headshots with me and I'm not here to give out autographs. Or take selfies, or whatever you kids are doing these days!" Olivia huffed. She pushed past them and into the hall, tossing a few blond curls over her shoulder.

"Autographs?" Bess asked, confused. "Autographs for what?"

"Oh, don't pretend you don't recognize me," Olivia said. "*Lonny and Jean*? *Heaven Will Help Me*? Six whole seasons of *The Garth Sisters*?"

When the girls didn't say anything, Olivia pulled down her sunglasses to show them her face. Nancy slowly understood. Olivia was famous. Nancy wasn't sure how, or why, but it was clear she thought they had seen her on television.

"I'm confused," George said. She glanced sideways at Bess, hoping she'd explain. Bess was the one who knew the most about television shows and pop culture. She'd read three different magazines on the plane.

Olivia looked around the hallway. "I know this place is a bit run-down, but I've been coming here for three decades. I'm attached to it."

"Oh, right . . . *The Garth Sisters*!" Bess said. "I've seen a million reruns of that show."

"Do you always come by yourself?" Nancy asked. She knew she couldn't admit that she didn't know who Olivia was, so she figured she'd sneak in as many questions as possible.

"Oh, I just come to get away from it all." Olivia sighed. "Usually, I bring Booboo, but now . . . this time . . ." She dabbed at her eyes.

"Who's Booboo?" Bess asked.

"My dear, beloved dog." Olivia rifled through her purse and pulled out a photo of a tan poodle in a red sweater. "He passed away just a week—"

She pulled a handful of tissues out of her purse, blew her nose, then pressed the photo to her heart. For a long while, the hallway was quiet.

"We actually wanted to talk to you about the luau last night," Bess started.

"I did *not* enjoy it," Olivia muttered. "I came

here for some privacy. To grieve my Booboo. And this *man* kept taking pictures of me."

"What did the man look like?" George asked. But the girls already knew the answer. Olivia must've thought Harry was photographing her. That's why she was acting so strange. She kept scowling at him because she thought he was trying to sneak pictures of her.

"He was bald," Olivia said. "And he was with his two teenagers. The worst part is, I would've taken a picture with him if he really wanted one. I'm not a monster!"

"Well, it was really nice to meet you," Nancy finally said. "And we're very sorry about Booboo."

"That's it? That's all you wanted to know?" Olivia laughed. "Most people at least ask about my relationship with Flynn Bigsby. He was a charming fellow. . . ."

"Maybe some other time," Bess said, hitting the button for the elevator. "We're sorry we bothered you, Ms. Andover."

As soon as the elevator doors opened, the girls slipped inside. They didn't say anything until they passed the third floor.

"So that solves that," George said. "She didn't steal Harry's camera. She just thought he was a crazy fan."

"I really did like *The Garth Sisters*," Bess added. "You'd think it was funny. It's about these two sisters who live in the Florida Keys, and they're always getting into trouble with their neighbors."

George frowned. "We never like the same shows."

"That's not true! You liked *The Magic Hour*!" Bess said.

"I hated *The Magic Hour*. It was so silly and—"

"She was our only suspect, so what now?" Nancy asked, interrupting them. She'd gotten really good at changing the subject when Bess and George started bickering. "The camera still hasn't shown up. If someone took it by accident, wouldn't they have returned it by now?"

"You're right," Bess said. "It definitely wasn't an accident. . . ."

The girls listened to a few more *bing*s as the elevator reached the bottom floor. For the first time in a long while, they were completely stumped.

Chapter

7

MYSTERY GIRL

Bess curled her knees to her chest. "I don't get it," she said. "It's like the camera vanished into thin air."

George took a bite of her french fry. "It must've been stolen when you and Harry were onstage. But I was too busy watching the show. I didn't see a single thing."

"And we were too busy hula-ing." Bess sighed.

Nancy looked out at the crystal-blue ocean. They were sitting on two lounge chairs on the

beach, enjoying some shade from a giant tiki umbrella. This was their last day of vacation, and they didn't have any real leads. Nancy thought back to the luau, and everything that had happened in those few minutes when she was onstage. Had she seen anything odd? Is it possible she'd missed a clue? She remembered following the hula dancers and seeing Carol smiling up at Harry, but that was it.

"Carol, Lizzy, and Z were all watching Harry," Nancy said. "And their seats were close to the stage, so the thief would've crept up behind them. . . ."

George took another french fry from the basket. They'd ordered a plate of chicken fingers for lunch, and they were going over what they knew about the case one more time, hoping for a breakthrough. "I bet most people were watching the hula show when the camera was taken," George said.

Surfers dove under the waves with their boards. A few toddlers were building sandcastles nearby while two redheaded children were having a handstand contest near the lifeguard station.

"Do those kids look familiar to you?" Bess pointed to three kids standing near the surf shack.

"Triplets," George said.

"Weren't they sitting near Harry at the luau?" Nancy asked.

"You're right!" Bess said. "That's exactly where I recognized them from."

"We should ask them if they saw anything," George said. "Maybe they're witnesses. One of them might have seen something during the show."

The girls left their half-eaten lunch and walked over to the surf shack. The triplets were there with their parents, who were returning two giant kayaks.

"Hi, Jordy!" Nancy called out to the green-haired teenager working at the shack. He rented out snorkels, kayaks, and surfboards, but he was also a really great surfer. He'd given the girls a surfing lesson on their first day at Sunrise Resort.

"Hey there! My shift is over soon, but let me know if you need another lesson before you go home. Practice makes perfect, yeah?" Jordy yelled over his shoulder as he helped the triplets' dad load the kayaks onto a rack.

"I think it would take ten more lessons for us to be perfect surfers," George whispered to

Nancy. It had been really hard to catch a wave. George had wiped out twice.

Bess turned to the triplets' mom. "I think I remember seeing you at the luau. Would you mind if we ask you some questions?"

The tall blond woman peeled off her life jacket. She wore a bright red one-piece bathing suit. "That should be fine. How can we help you?"

"Did you guys see anything strange last night?" George asked.

One of the boys smiled. He held a finger up and started talking excitedly. "Everything was strange, because strange is just another word for different! And it all was so different that night. I'd never seen the hula or a fire dancer before!"

His brother and sister were much quieter. They stood off to the side, watching him talk.

"We think someone might have stolen a camera," Bess explained. "Did you see anyone holding one? Maybe they were walking fast or seemed like they were hiding something?"

"I love cameras," the first triplet said. His green

eyes got much bigger, and he smiled again. "Last summer, I took a photography class at the community center and my teacher, Chuck, showed me how to change the aperture setting, which controls how much light you let into the camera. Then he taught me about shutter speed. That's how the camera captures motion."

"You love cameras?" Nancy asked. She glanced sideways at Bess and George. Was it possible this kid was a suspect? Did he like cameras so much, he'd take one that wasn't his?

"Oh, I would have a million if I could," he continued.

"Do you remember seeing any cool cameras at the luau last night?" George asked. It was a trick, of course. If the boy said no, they'd know he was lying. If he said yes, he might reveal some more clues they'd missed.

"This man with a shiny bald head had the coolest camera. It was super expensive. I think it was a Bluestone 5400, but I'm not totally sure."

Nancy perked up. Not only was this boy sitting at the table next to Harry when the camera went missing, but he'd been admiring it. Had he liked it enough that he wanted it for himself?

His mom stepped forward, her arms crossed over her chest. She didn't look happy. "What's this about? A camera went missing, so you want to blame Timmy? Everyone's heard the rumors, you know."

"What rumors?" George asked.

The father left the kayaks on the rack and came toward them, his brow furrowed. He didn't look happy either. He wrapped his arms around his three children, bringing them closer to him. "Some teenager took it. People saw her on the beach with it this morning. Meanwhile, that man and his wife are going around questioning everyone at the resort. We're on vacation. We don't need this!"

Nancy pulled her clue book from her back pocket and started scribbling down notes. "I'm so sorry . . . but maybe you could just tell us a little about the teenager? Did you see her yourselves?"

"We didn't," the mom said. She pulled her glossy blond hair into a ponytail. "But I heard people talking about her. I think they said she had glasses and black hair?"

"No, no. They said she was tall and had brown hair," the father said. "It was in a ponytail?"

"She was wearing purple sneakers," the mom interrupted.

"Yes, that I remember," the dad agreed. "I definitely heard she was wearing purple sneakers."

Nancy underlined *PURPLE SNEAKERS*. She wasn't surprised that the mom and dad remembered the description differently. It was hard to get people to agree on what they saw or heard. But they both had said that the girl with the camera had been wearing purple sneakers. That seemed like a big clue.

"Anything else?" George asked. "Can you point us to the people who saw her?"

"Oh, I don't remember who we were talking to," the dad said. He waved off into the distance. "I actually heard several different people talking about it. They were somewhere down the beach."

"Thank you, and thanks, Timmy!" Bess called over their shoulder. Then the Clue Crew took off to find their first real witnesses.

Chapter

THEY'RE HIDING SOMETHING

The girls didn't get very far before they saw Z, Harry's son. He was standing by the water, talking to Jordy, who'd just finished up his shift at the surf shack. They both had surfboards tucked under their arms.

"That sizzle reel is going to be awesome," Jordy said. "I don't care if five hundred people want to be in this competition. With that tape, I've got a serious chance."

"No doubt!" Z gave Jordy a high five, then

they bumped their fists. "Big Island Surfers, here you come. Now, we just have to find someone to put it all together."

"What competition?" George asked. The girls stopped and let the water rush over their toes. A few yards out, a surfer rode in on a huge wave.

"Oh, just this surfing contest Jordy's trying to get into," Z said. He ran his hand through his fauxhawk. "Did you find out anything about my dad's camera? He's still really upset, but I have a feeling it'll turn up somewhere."

"We do have one clue," Nancy said. "People are saying they saw a girl with it on the beach this morning. We're not totally sure what she looks like, but we know she was wearing purple sneakers."

"Does that sound familiar?" Bess asked.

Jordy stared out at the ocean and shrugged. "Uh . . . I don't think so?"

"What do you mean?" George said. It was a simple question. Had they seen a girl with purple sneakers or not?

"Nah, doesn't sound familiar," Z said. He turned back to Jordy. "You want to catch a few waves?"

Then the two sprinted into the ocean, shouting "Good luck!" and "Bye!" to Nancy and her friends. Bess and George just stood there and stared after them.

"That was weird," Bess finally said.

"It was like they didn't want to talk to us," Nancy agreed.

The friends walked down the beach, past the kids making sandcastles. A toddler stomped on a few, and a girl with pigtails burst into tears. Not far down the beach from where Jordy and Z had been talking, the Clue Crew found another group of teenagers lying on blankets—a girl wearing a striped bikini, two boys in wet suits pulled down to their waists, and a guy with a nose ring. There were three surfboards next to them.

"I'm Nancy, and these are my friends Bess and George. Did you guys happen to see a girl wearing purple sneakers today?" Nancy asked. "Maybe this morning?"

The girl in the striped bikini looked up at them. "Why do you want to know?"

Nancy wasn't sure what to say. She didn't want to lie. "We think she might know something about a missing camera."

"I don't want to get anyone in trouble." The girl shook her head. "That wouldn't be cool."

Bikini Girl lay back down on her towel and closed her eyes. The two wet-suit boys shrugged, but they didn't seem like they were going to answer, either. The boy with the nose ring was staring at them like he wanted to say something, but after a minute passed, Nancy and her friends all felt a bit silly. The teenagers were ignoring them.

"Let's go, Nancy. . . ." George tugged on Nancy's arm.

As soon as the girls were sure the teens couldn't hear them, they started talking about the case.

"They're protecting someone!" Bess said. "That was just like what happened with Z and Jordy. They know who took they camera, but they don't want to get them in trouble."

"I think you're right," Nancy said.

George shook her head, annoyed. "Whoever took the camera must be a surfer. Z, Jordy, and those teenagers—they're all surfers."

"Maybe," Bess said. "Or they're close friends with the surfers. I bet they're all around the same age."

The girls kept walking down the beach toward a family a few yards ahead. They'd have to question people who weren't surfers if they were going to get any real answers. As they passed a beach volleyball game, the trio heard something behind them. It sounded like someone was running.

"Hey! Wait up!" a voice called out.

When they turned around, they saw the boy with the nose ring crossing the sand toward them. He had dark, almond-shaped eyes and was wearing neon-green board shorts. He glanced over his shoulder, like he didn't want anyone to see him talking with the Clue Crew.

"I'm Ben," he said. "I'm sorry about before. Gina was a little rude."

"Who's she protecting?" Nancy asked.

Ben seemed uncomfortable with the question. He just shrugged and pointed to a figure in the distance, "Look . . . you should ask her about the camera."

Nancy, Bess, and George squinted against the sun. They could barely see the person he was motioning to. But before they could ask him anything else, he ran back the way he came, returning to his friends.

"Thanks?" Bess called after him. She wasn't even sure what she was thanking him for. What did the girl know? Why did Ben want them to talk to her?

They picked up their pace, walking twice as fast as before, trying to catch up to the girl. As they got closer, they saw she was barefoot.

"I don't get it!" George said. "Why is this person so important? She's not the girl with the purple sneakers."

"But look," Nancy said. She pointed to the bag the girl was holding—a little black backpack with something tied to the front of it.

Bess and George looked closer, and noticed there was a pair of purple high-tops tied to the bag. They swung back and forth as she walked.

"The girl with the purple sneakers!" Bess said excitedly. "It *is* her!"

Chapter

9

THE CHASE

Nancy, Bess, and George followed the girl down the beach, trying to stay close enough so she was always in view. It was hard, though. The beach was crowded. Every now and then, a group of surfers would get in their way. The Clue Crew almost lost sight of the girl when a skinny boy with dreadlocks dove right in front of them. He hit a volleyball up into the air just before it landed in the sand.

"We need to get closer," George said. "We're going to lose her!"

Their suspect was just a tiny figure at the very end of the beach now. The girls started running, swerving through picnic blankets and lounge chairs, and past a bunch of umbrellas made of straw. When the sand got too crowded, they went down to the water, racing through the waves and soaking the bottoms of their shorts.

"There she is!" Nancy called out. They could

see her more clearly now. She had on a white base-ball cap and a long, flowy dress.

But as Nancy, Bess, and George closed in, the girl with the purple sneakers must have sensed something was wrong. She turned around, but it was hard to see her face. She was wearing huge black sunglasses.

"Is she looking at us?" Bess asked as the girls paused to catch their breath.

For a few seconds, the girl with the purple sneakers didn't move. But then, without a word, she turned again and ran as fast as she could in the opposite direction.

"She's trying to get away!" George yelled. The Clue Crew sprinted after her, but it felt like their feet were sinking. They ran half the speed they normally would have, every step difficult in the sand as they wound through more beach umbrellas.

The girl was heading toward a crowded restaurant with tables overlooking the water.

When they got closer, Nancy realized there was a wedding going on. A hundred people were eating and dancing, all dressed up in suits and long gowns.

The girl ran through the flowered archway and into the party, disappearing into the crowd of guests. A few older couples twirled around the dance floor. Dozens of waiters were passing appetizers on shiny silver trays.

"Quick, this way!" Nancy ran around the side of the patio. Then Nancy, Bess, and George slipped through a small gate, unnoticed, before sneaking around two waiters with trays full of drinks. But the girls were so much shorter than everyone else, and they couldn't see their suspect anymore.

A tuxedoed man stepped forward holding a microphone. "And now, I'd like to introduce . . . the new Mr. and Mrs. Garcia!"

The bride and groom strolled out through the restaurant's glass doors. Mrs. Garcia was wearing a beautiful poufy white dress and a flower in her hair. Music started playing, and Mr. Garcia took her hand to dance. Normally, Nancy and her friends would've loved to watch, but now they could see the girl with the purple sneakers on the other side of the patio, ducking out of the party and racing down the street.

The Clue Crew was stuck. They couldn't run across the dance floor and ruin the couple's first dance, so they just stood there, watching as their suspect made her escape. When the dance was finally over, they snuck out of the side gate and ran to the street, where they saw a long strip of shops and restaurants stretched out behind the beach. They didn't see the girl anywhere.

"She got away," Bess said sadly. "She's gone."

"She's definitely the one who took the camera," George added, "or she wouldn't have run. Now that she knows we're looking for her, she's going to be super careful. We probably won't ever see her again."

Nancy looked up and down the street one last time, hoping the girl would reappear.

How were they going to find Harry's camera when their only suspect had vanished?

Chapter

10

A SURPRISE FOR HARRY

"You tried your best," Mrs. Fayne said. She took a bite of her mahi-mahi. "That's all that matters. Some mysteries aren't meant to be solved."

"Like what happened on Amelia Earhart's final flight," Mr. Fayne said.

"Or the Loch Ness monster," Mrs. Fayne added. "They still don't know if that picture is a fake or not. There are people who still swear that monster exists."

"Monster?" Scotty asked. His eyes went wide

as he pushed some rice around with his fork.

"But we know it's not real," Mr. Fayne said under his breath. "Monsters don't exist!"

"This isn't anything like the Loch Ness monster," George said, annoyed. "We know who took Harry's camera. We just don't know where to find her."

Nancy rested her chin in her hands. It was their last dinner in Hawaii, and Mr. and Mrs. Fayne had spent most of it trying to make Nancy, Bess, and George feel better about losing their suspect. They'd fly home tomorrow morning and they'd never know what happened to the camera. As happy as Nancy would be to see her dad, she couldn't believe they'd come so close to solving this mystery . . . and then hadn't.

Mrs. Fayne tried again. "We're just saying, it's okay. You girls did a great job. You chased that suspect into a wedding!"

Bess started laughing, and before long, Nancy and George couldn't help but join in. Soon, they were all laughing so hard their stomachs hurt.

Chasing a suspect through a wedding was definitely silly, to say the least.

"We crashed a wedding!" Bess giggled. Nancy had heard that term from some older kids. It basically meant they went to a party they weren't invited to.

"Girls! We have some really big news!" a familiar voice called out.

Nancy turned to see the Hendrickses striding through the restaurant. Then she noticed the strangest thing—Harry was holding his camera.

"We found the camera!" Carol said excitedly, clapping her hands together.

"Oh my gosh! Where?" Nancy asked. Was it possible the Clue Crew had been wrong? Maybe the girl hadn't stolen it. . . .

"Well, I guess it found us," Harry said, holding the camera tight. "We were in our room, getting ready for dinner, and this note slid under our door. It said, 'Your camera is right outside.' That's all."

"And when we opened the door, it was!" Carol

said. She hadn't stopped smiling since she'd walked into the restaurant. "It was just sitting there on the ground. We looked up and down the hall, but we didn't see anyone. I don't know who returned it, but I'm just so relieved."

Nancy looked at Bess and George. They both seemed as confused as she was.

"What do you mean?" Nancy asked. "Were there any new pictures on there? Anything to

tell you who had it for the last two days?"

"The camera was wiped clean. No photos or videos," Harry said. He held up a small black piece of plastic. "But they did put all our old photos and videos on this separate drive. Everything from the fiftieth anniversary party—it's all there!"

"Well, that's terrific news," Mr. Fayne said. He gave George the smallest nudge. "Isn't it, girls?"

Nancy and her friends were too stunned to respond. Maybe Harry had gotten his camera back, but the story sounded so strange. Why would someone go through all that trouble stealing a camera, only to return it two days later? Why would they save all the pictures and videos on it? And how did they know where Harry's room was?

"It is terrific," Nancy said. "But also confusing. Would you mind if we look at that note?"

Harry and Carol shrugged. Now that their camera was back, they didn't seem to care about who'd taken it in the first place.

"Sure, it's in our room." Harry waved his hand. "Follow me."

· · ·

The Hendrickses' room was on the second floor of the hotel, overlooking a garden. The first thing Nancy noticed was that room 208 was right in the middle of the floor. You had to walk at least thirty seconds to get to either staircase. How did the person drop the camera off and get away so quickly?

"I don't think they could have jumped over the railing," Bess said, resting her hands on it. It was almost as tall as she was. "Too high, and too big a fall. Maybe they ran to the staircase. Or maybe the note was there for a while."

Carol opened their door and pointed to a dressing table right inside. "No, I was sitting right there. I remember seeing the paper come under the door. It was probably less than a minute between when I saw the note and I checked the hall."

"Did you hear anything strange? Like footsteps? Or someone running?" George asked.

"Nope," Harry said. "Lizzy or Z might have. You can ask them. They're right next door in two-oh-seven."

The Hendrickses' room was very similar to the one George's parents were staying in. It had one big bed in the middle of one wall. Harry's shirts were piled on a chair in the corner. Carol's makeup was laid out on the dressing table, along with a stack of magazines.

"Here it is." Carol grabbed the note from the nightstand and handed it to Nancy.

The girls all stared at the sheet. It was the same Sunrise Resort stationery that was in every room. The note was written in all lowercase letters, but other than that, Nancy didn't see anything unusual about it.

"Can we keep this?" Bess asked. When Carol nodded, she tucked it in her back pocket. "We'll go next door and ask Lizzy and Z if they heard anything. No matter what, we're glad you got your camera back."

"Me too," Harry said cheerfully. "What a night!"

Nancy slipped out of the hotel room and knocked on the door of room 207. Bess and George were right behind her. After a few moments, Z opened the door. His fauxhawk was messy, like he hadn't put gel in it yet.

"What's up?" he said. "Did you guys hear my dad found his camera?"

"Yeah," Bess said. "We were wondering if you heard anything strange tonight. . . . Someone running down the hall, maybe?"

Z shook his head. "Nah . . ."

From where the girls were standing, they could see Lizzy was on her phone, lying on one of the beds with her earphones in. The room was much messier than their parents' room.

Out of the corner of her eye, Nancy saw a plastic package sticking up out of the trash can. She suddenly had an idea.

"Ah, I guess we should all just be happy it turned up, right?" she asked.

"Think so," Z agreed.

"Just one last thing. Mind if we borrow a piece of paper?"

Z shrugged. He went back into the room and ripped a piece of paper off the Sunrise Resort notepad on the desk, then handed it to Nancy.

"Thanks," she said before he closed the door.

"What's that for?" Bess asked, staring at the blank paper. "We have the same notepad back in our room."

"I think I know who returned the camera," Nancy said. "The same person who took it in the first place."

Clue Crew—and YOU!

Can you see the whole picture and figure out who the camera culprit might be? Try thinking like the Clue Crew. Or keep reading to find out who the thief is!

1. The Clue Crew ruled out Olivia Andover as a suspect. Can you think of other people at the resort who might have stolen the camera? Using a pen and paper, write down any suspects the Clue Crew may have overlooked.

2. When Nancy sees Lizzy and Z's notepad, she gets an idea. How could that single piece of paper help solve the mystery? Write down your thoughts.

3. The Clue Crew thinks it's strange that Harry and Carol didn't see anyone in the hallway when they found the camera. Write down three possible reasons for this.

Chapter

11

A HIDDEN MESSAGE

Nancy led her friends to the computer lab next to the lobby. She knew she probably should've told them what she was so excited about, but she wanted to *show* them instead. While Bess and George sat down in front of a computer, Nancy borrowed a pencil from the front desk. Then she went to work.

"I needed a piece of paper from Lizzy and Z's notepad," Nancy said, "so I could see the last note they wrote on it."

She rubbed the side of the pencil against the paper, slowly revealing the marks left from the last note that had been written on the pad. After a minute or so, the words *your camera is outside your door* appeared like magic. Bess covered her mouth with her hand.

"Lizzy and Z were the ones who wrote that note," George said. "They're the ones who stole Harry's camera."

Bess nodded. "It wouldn't be hard to get away if you just had to walk right next door. They

must've put the camera down, slipped the note under their parents' door, and run back to their own room."

"But why?" Nancy said. "That's the real question. Let's look up 'sizzle reel.' I think it might have something to do with what Z and Jordy were talking about on the beach."

George typed away, pulling up a web page. "According to this site, a sizzle reel is a short video, like a highlight reel you use to promote yourself."

"Promote yourself?" Bess asked.

"For example, if you want to enter a surfing competition . . ." George's eyes went wide. "That's what happened! Lizzy and Z were helping Jordy make a video to enter the Big Island Surfer contest. Harry's camera is top-of-the-line. It would be a much better video than anything you could record on a cell phone."

Nancy stared down at the note. Now that she thought about it, she remembered that Lizzy had been wearing purple high-tops at the luau. She'd been the girl who ran away from them on the beach. She must have panicked and returned the camera right after.

"We have to tell Carol and Harry. . . ." Nancy said.

The girls shared a nervous look. Carol and Harry Hendricks had seemed so happy before. Now the Clue Crew was going to have to tell them their kids had stolen the camera? That Lizzy and Z had been lying to them the whole time? What would they say?

Nancy, Bess, and George walked into the Green Pineapple just as the Hendrickses were finishing up their dinner. Now that Harry had his camera back, he was taking dozens of pictures again. He knelt down in front of Z and Lizzy and kept trying to get them to smile.

Nancy took a deep breath before approaching their table. "We found out who took the camera. But do you really want to know?"

"Well, yes," Harry said. "If there's a thief on the loose, they should be reported to the manager and never be allowed at Sunrise Resort again!"

Nancy looked at Lizzy and Z. Both their faces had turned bright red. Nancy was hoping they would reveal the truth so she didn't have to. Just as she was about to speak, Lizzy jumped in.

"Dad . . . it was us. Z and I took your camera. We needed it to help a friend we met on the beach."

"What?" Carol asked. She put down her fork. "You took the camera? You're kidding, right?"

"But why?" Harry asked. His face had gone pale. "We've been searching everywhere for it and you didn't say anything?"

"Our friend, Jordy, he wanted to enter this surfing contest, but all he had was this flip phone," Z explained. "And we wanted to make him this amazing highlight reel so he'd be picked as a contestant. Even the video on our phones wasn't that great, so we thought if we used your—"

"Then you should have asked." Harry's brow furrowed. He was just as flustered as he'd been at the luau when he found out the camera was missing. "This is how you thank me for taking you on a nice vacation? You steal my camera and lie to me and your mother? When were you going to tell us the truth?"

Lizzy rolled her eyes. She was about to say something, but her mom interrupted her.

"Do not roll your eyes, young lady." She pointed a finger at Lizzy. "You and your brother are in big trouble once we get home."

"But, Dad," Lizzy started, "we *did* ask to borrow your camera. Three times. It's like you didn't hear a word we said. You're obsessed with that thing. You kept taking a thousand pictures and telling us to pose or smile. It's like you've barely talked to us since we got here."

Harry's face softened. "I don't think that's true. And if it is, I certainly didn't mean to ignore you."

"We know what we did was wrong," Z said, "but we were just trying to help a friend. Jordy's one of the best surfers on this island. He had to get into that contest."

"It was wrong. Very, very wrong," Carol said. But this time, her voice was gentler.

"I really didn't think I was ignoring you," Harry said. "You kids are my whole world. I only wanted to come here for you so we could all spend some time together."

Carol turned to the Clue Crew. "Thank you for your help. We'll take it from here."

Nancy and her friends went back to Mr. and Mrs. Fayne's table. While they'd been gone, the Faynes had ordered pineapple ice cream for dessert, along with a giant slice of haupia cake. The girls grabbed the extra forks and dug in.

"Looks like we solved the mystery after all," George said.

Nancy laughed. "Yeah, this was no Loch Ness monster."

"Monster?!" Scotty said through a mouthful of cake. "I don't like monsters. . . ."

"Not a real monster," Mr. Fayne explained.

"You'll have to tell us the whole story. But for now, let's celebrate another case solved!"

Mrs. Fayne said. She held a spoonful of ice cream in the air, pretending to toast with it. The girls smiled and held up their own spoonfuls of cake and ice cream.

Their last night on Hawaii had truly been their best.

Test your detective skills with even more Clue Book mysteries:

Nancy Drew Clue Book #15: The Great Goat Gaffe

"What could be better than spring break?" George Fayne asked.

"Spring break and spring clothes?" Bess Marvin said.

Eight-year-old Nancy Drew smiled at her two best friends. "Spring break and feeding goats here at Sweet Creams Farm!" she declared.

It was a sunny Tuesday in early spring. Nancy, Bess, and George were often busy solving mysteries as the Clue Crew. This day, they were busy volunteering at Sweet Creams Farm.

To the girls, Sweet Creams was the best farm

ever. Not only did it sell goat cheese, yogurt, and ice cream, but it had its own petting zoo filled with tiny pygmy goats!

"Hey, you guys!" George chuckled as three goats tried to drink out of the bottle she clutched. "One per customer!"

But the goats at Sweet Creams weren't only for feeding or for petting. They were part of a cool new class at Sweet Creams—goat yoga!

"Feeding tiny goats is super fun," Nancy said as they carefully placed empty bottles in a wooden crate, "but I wish we could join a real-live goat yoga class."

"Yoga is supposed to be so relaxing!" Bess added.

"What's relaxing about twisting yourself into a pretzel while goats climb all over you?" George asked. "If you ask me, I'd rather play soccer."

The three friends left the pen to make room for the goat yoga class. Women and men chatted excitedly as they laid their mats on the soft grassy ground. Some curious goats were already wandering around the mats, bleating softly.

Nancy, Bess, and George watched through the fence as the yoga instructor, Nina Pickles, began the class. Besides teaching yoga, Nina had her own store where she sold activewear and workout clothes.

"Be one with the goats as we enter the low lunge," Nina told the class. "And be sure to check out the low sale prices at Nina Pickles Activewear. This week only!"

Nancy, Bess, and George traded smiles. Nina was always looking for ways to spread the word about her store.

"Let's lie on our stomachs for the cobra pose," Nina instructed. "Cobra, as in the new snake-skin-design leggings just in at my store!"

"Baaaaa!" one of the tiny goats bleated as he scampered onto a posing man's back.

"Pygmy goats are as small as puppies," Bess pointed out. "It's hard to tell which ones are the babies."

"*You mean kids*," George said. "We learned

here on the farm that baby goats are called kids, remember?"

Kids! The word made Nancy's eyes light up.

"Bess, George, the most awesome idea just popped into my head! What if Sweet Creams Farm had a goat yoga class for kids?"

"You mean human kids, like us?" Bess asked.

"Yes," Nancy said. "The class can be called . . . Kids with Kids!"

"Cool!" Bess exclaimed.

"Cool for other kids," George said as they watched a goat crawl onto a woman's shoulder. "Like I said, I'll stick to soccer."

"I bet you'll like goat yoga too, George." Nancy giggled. "Let's find Sophie and see what she thinks."

Sophie Sweet was the energetic woman who ran Sweet Creams Farm. Nancy, Bess, and George found her at the farm stand unpacking bottles of goat milk smoothies.

After hearing Nancy's idea, she smiled. "A goat yoga class for kids would be great for Sweet

Creams Farm," she said. "And for *Wake Up River Heights!*"

"*Wake Up River Heights?*" Nancy repeated. "You mean the TV show that's on super early in the morning?"

"Correct!" Sophie said. "A crew is coming to the farm tomorrow morning to film our goat yoga class." Sophie gave an excited little hop. "With spring break this week, a goat yoga class just for kids would be perfect!"

"Oooh!" a voice exclaimed. "Perfect for me, too!"

The girls turned to see Nina Pickles, a towel draped over one shoulder.

"Why aren't you with your class, Nina?" Sophie asked.

"I left them in the deep relaxation pose," Nina explained, "but who can relax with news about a goat yoga class for kids?"

Nancy couldn't believe her ears. "You like my idea too, Ms. Pickles?" she asked.

"Sure I do!" Nina said. "I'm unveiling my new line of kids activewear this week. What better time to introduce it than on TV?"

"Oh," Sophie said, hesitating. "I'm afraid that's not a good idea, Nina."

"Why not?" Nina asked, surprised.

"*Wake Up River Heights* wants to cover goat yoga," Sophie explained, "not fashion."

Nina gasped. "Everything is about fashion, Sophie!" She closed her eyes and took deep breaths through her nose before adding, "I think you'd better find another yoga instructor for tomorrow."

The girls watched as Sophie huffed back to the goat yoga pen and her class.

"Will Nina be okay, Sophie?" Nancy asked. "She seemed very upset."

"She'll get over it, I'm sure," Sophie said. "In the meantime, I have an important job for you girls."

"A job?" Bess gulped. "You don't want us to clean the goat pen, do you?"

"No, Bess." Sophie chuckled. "I need you to find kids for our goat yoga class tomorrow. They need to be here at seven thirty sharp."

"No problem, Sophie," Nancy said quickly. "We have lots of friends and classmates to invite."

"Getting them to be on TV will be easy," George added.

"Easier than cleaning the goat pen!" Bess said, clearly relieved.

"Good! I'll get some permission slips to give to your friends," Sophie said. "Tell them to bring their slip signed by a parent tomorrow."

Sophie went to her office for the permission slips.

The girls couldn't wait to find kids for the goat yoga class!

"I am soooo excited!" Bess said. Then, "What are we going to wear to the goat yoga class?"

"Goat footprints," George joked.

Nancy smiled and said, "As soon as we get the permission slips, let's go to Main Street. We'll find lots of kids there."

Nancy, Bess, and George all had the same rules. They could walk anywhere, as long as it was under five blocks—and as long as they were together. Together was more fun anyway.

When the girls reached Main Street, they found lots of kids they knew. But most of the kids knew nothing about yoga. . . .

"I like frozen yoga," Peter Patino said, pointing to the nearby fro-yo shop. "Will they have chocolate or strawberry?"

Some kids had heard about yoga, but not goat yoga. When the girls invited Kendra Jackson, she asked, "Are the goats gentle?"

George nodded. "You won't know there's a goat on your back," she explained, "until you smell the hay on its breath!"

"Ew," Kendra said, wrinkling her nose.

When the girls asked Henderson Murphy, he shook his head. "I watch *Danger Dog* at that time every morning," he said. "Tomorrow is the flea circus episode."

"You'd rather watch TV than be on TV?" George groaned. "Whatever!"

The girls left Henderson and walked up Main Street. When they ran out of kids to invite, they turned onto Magnolia Street.

"I don't blame Henderson for wanting to see *Danger Dog* tomorrow," Bess said. "The flea circus episode rocks."

"What if *everybody* wants to watch *Danger Dog* tomorrow morning?" George asked, imagining the worst. "What if no one shows up?"

Nancy wasn't too worried. "Some kids said yes, some said no, and a few said maybe," she stated. "Let's hope for the best."

The three friends were about to make their way home when—*"Baaaaa! Baaaaa! Baaaaa!"*

Nancy, Bess, and George froze. Had they just heard what they thought they'd heard?

"Was that . . . a goat?" Nancy asked.

"For sure," George said, looking around. "After being at the farm all day, I know a goat when I hear one."

"Except we're not on the farm," Bess said. "We're on Magnolia Street."

The girls followed the sound to the middle of the block. George pointed to a green house with white shutters. "It's coming from the Dishers' house," she said.

Eight-year-old Leslie Disher was in the girls' class at school. Leslie loved writing in her journal. She also worshipped teen singing idol, Brad Sylvester. Nancy, Bess, and George didn't know Leslie's twin brother, Wesley, as well. He was in the other third-grade class.

"*Baaaaaaa!*"

The bleating grew louder as Nancy, Bess, and George followed it to the backyard. A big trampoline was set up there. But it wasn't Leslie or Wesley jumping up and down on it. It was a tiny brown-and-white pygmy goat!

"*Baaaa! Baaaa!*" the goat bleated as it bounced sky-high. The girls couldn't believe their eyes as they watched the goat perform awesome front flips and backflips and midair spins!

"That's a goat all right," Nancy said.

"Not just any goat, Nancy!" George said with a grin. "That's *Pogo*!"

Nancy Drew

✶ CLUE BOOK ✶

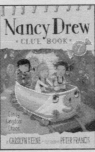

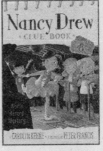

Test your
detective skills with
Nancy and her best
friends, Bess and
George!

NancyDrew.com

EBOOK EDITIONS ALSO AVAILABLE
From Aladdin ✶ simonandschuster.com/kids

FOLLOW THE TRAIL AND SOLVE MYSTERIES WITH FRANK AND JOE!

HardyBoysSeries.com

Looking for another great book?
Find it
IN THE MIDDLE.

Fun, fantastic books for kids
in the in-be**TWEEN** age.

IntheMiddleBooks.com

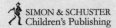